Follow That Egg!

adapted by Catherine Lukas
illustrated by The Artifact Group

Ready-to-Read

SCHOLASTIC INC.
New York Toronto London Auckland Sydney
Mexico City New Delhi Hong Kong Buenos Aires

ISBN-13: 978-0-545-04177-5
ISBN-10: 0-545-04177-5

12 11 10 9 8 7 6 5 4 3 2 1   8 9 10 11 12 13/0

Printed in the U.S.A.

First Scholastic printing, March 2008

"Look! King has

PABLO

a job for us," says .

TYRONE

"Ready, Knight ?"

UNIQUA

"Ready, Sir !"

TYRONE

"I know! Maybe King  PABLO

needs us to go up DRAGON MOUNTAIN,"

says Knight UNIQUA.

"We knights do not mind

a big job.

We might even see a ,"
DRAGON

says Sir .
TYRONE

"Brave knights, I must go

to the  store.
CROWN

I need a new ,"
CROWN

says King  .
PABLO

"Your job is to take care of this  EGG while I am gone. Please keep the EGG safe and sound."

"An ?" asks   .

EGG   UNIQUA

"An   does not move

EGG

at all," says   .

TYRONE

"   would be more

DRAGON MOUNTAIN

interesting."

The starts to roll.
EGG

The rolls away.
EGG

"Stop that ! "
EGG

yells Knight .
UNIQUA

The  rolls
EGG

down the 📶 ,
STEPS

through the 🚪 ,
DOOR

and into the 〰️ .
WATER

The  floats to the EGG FOREST of the Grabbing Goblin.

"The Grabbing Goblin

will grab the !" says
EGG

Knight .
UNIQUA

"Watch out!"

Someone grabs

their ,
HELMETS

their ,
SHIELDS

and then the !
EGG

"Grabbing Goblin!"

says Knight .
UNIQUA

"Give back that !"
EGG

It is too late.

They all go over

the  .

WATERFALL

Hooray! They catch the  !

EGG

Crack!

Now the  has  !

EGG   LEGS

The  runs away.

EGG

They pass the Fairy .

HOUSE

Fairy TASHA wants the EGG too!

She tries to take it.

Crack!

Now the has !
EGG WINGS

The flies away.
EGG

It flies up .
DRAGON MOUNTAIN

"The  is in danger!"
EGG

says Fairy ⬚ .
TASHA

"Oh, no! What if a ⬚ gets it?"
DRAGON

asks Sir ⬚ .
TYRONE

"We have to save the ⬚ !"
EGG

At the top of  DRAGON MOUNTAIN,

Sir TYRONE finds an empty

shell. Did the EGG hatch?

"Ah! A DRAGON !" yells AUSTIN.

"Run!"

They run. Then they fall.

A baby  catches them.

DRAGON

"Look what hatched from

the !"

EGG

says Knight .

UNIQUA

"We have to show the king!"

says Sir .

TYRONE

King  returns.

PABLO

He has a new .

CROWN

"I see the  hatched,"

EGG

he says.

"I hope it was no trouble."

"Not for brave knights like us!"

says Sir .

TYRONE

"Good," says King .

PABLO

"I knew you could do the job.

Come to my 🏰 for a snack!"

PALACE